Furry Mouse

Written by Tiffany Joyner
Illustrated by Jose Antonio Acosta

Published by InkDrops Publishing, LLC and Brown Brainy Brilliant Books
ISBN: 978-1-7337947-4-9

To my father, John Joyner,
who instilled in me the appreciation for a good story.

To my mother, Shirley Joyner,
who encouraged me to create my own.

Furry Mouse, Furry Mouse
PLEASE--
Leave me and my little house!

GO ON!
Take these vittles
And visit my neighbors a little.
They truly like your kind
And I surely wouldn't mind.

Furry Mouse, Furry Mouse
PLEASE--
Leave me and my little house!

I have nothing more to share,
My cabinets are bare.
You REALLY give me a terrible scare!

Look!
Nothing on the floor,
So I'll just open the
door--

And you can see your
way out.
I'll show you the
route!

Furry Mouse, Furry Mouse
PLEASE--
Leave me and my little house!

I'll trap a skunk
To scent the air.

Come out your hole?
You wouldn't dare!

Furry Mouse, Furry Mouse
PLEASE--
Leave me and my little house!

Oh no, a pair!
You brought along a friend to share!
Go away!
You give me a scare!

Here's some yummy cheese
And peanut butter to wash it down.
Just be quiet!
Don't make a sound.

Furry Mouse, Furry Mouse
I packed my bags.
Left the house.

Furry Mouse, Oh Furry Mouse
I moved into another house.
You can find it if you seek,
Will you come and take a peek?

Come on over!
Meet my friend, Josie.
She's eager to meet you,
She's just as nosy.

Josie will greet you.
She'll know your smell...

Tiffany Joyner is originally from Brooklyn, New York, but currently resides in Pennsylvania. She is a playwright with three productions under her belt which have had successful performances in Philadelphia, New Jersey, and Washington D.C.
"Furry Mouse" is her first picture book for children which uses humor to address fear, while also finding positive solutions to combat our struggles.

   Other projects include a YA book called "What Nana Left". It explores the timeless pieces of wisdom left to us by our grandmothers. In addition to her literary pursuits, she is also an educator and founder of "Write Away". This literacy-based initiative was created in July 2019 to address the engagement challenges that our schools face in the areas of reading and writing. The program uses a combination of creative workshops and seminars for children and their families to develop and improve literacy skills.

Jose Antonio Acosta Perez was born in Havana, Cuba. He graduated from San Alejandro Academy of Fine Arts in 1999. His paintings have been exhibited in different cities, such as Sidney, Australia; Shanghai, China; Toronto, Canada and La Habana, Cuba.

With more than 25 years of expertise as an illustrator, he has done illustrations for prominent publishing houses in Cuba and abroad, such as Editorial Gente Nueva (Cuba), Editorial Union (Cuba), Ferilibro (Dominican Republic), and Isla Negra Ediciones (Puerto Rico). His illustrations have also been included in several specialized exhibitions.

Made in the USA
Middletown, DE
20 October 2020